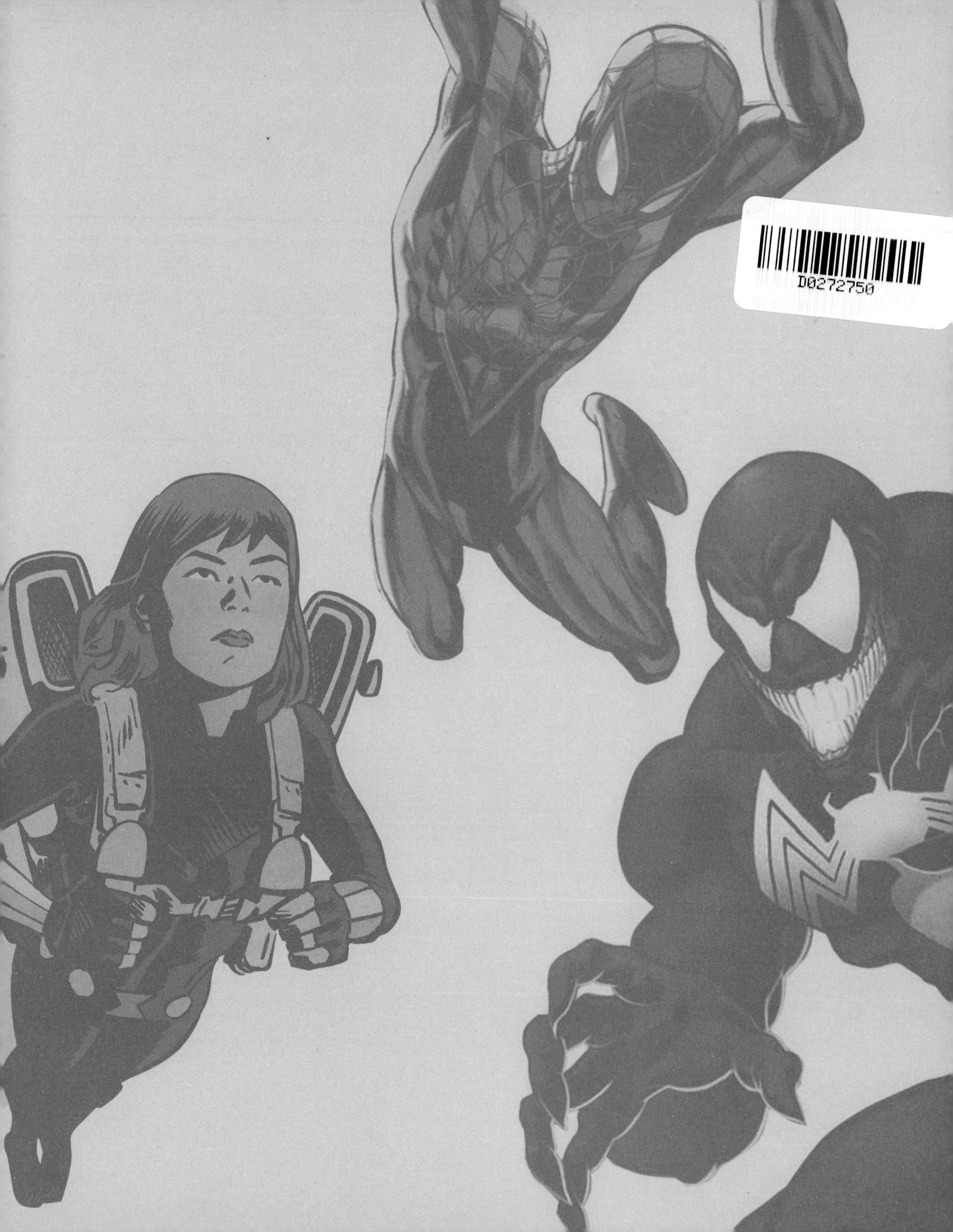

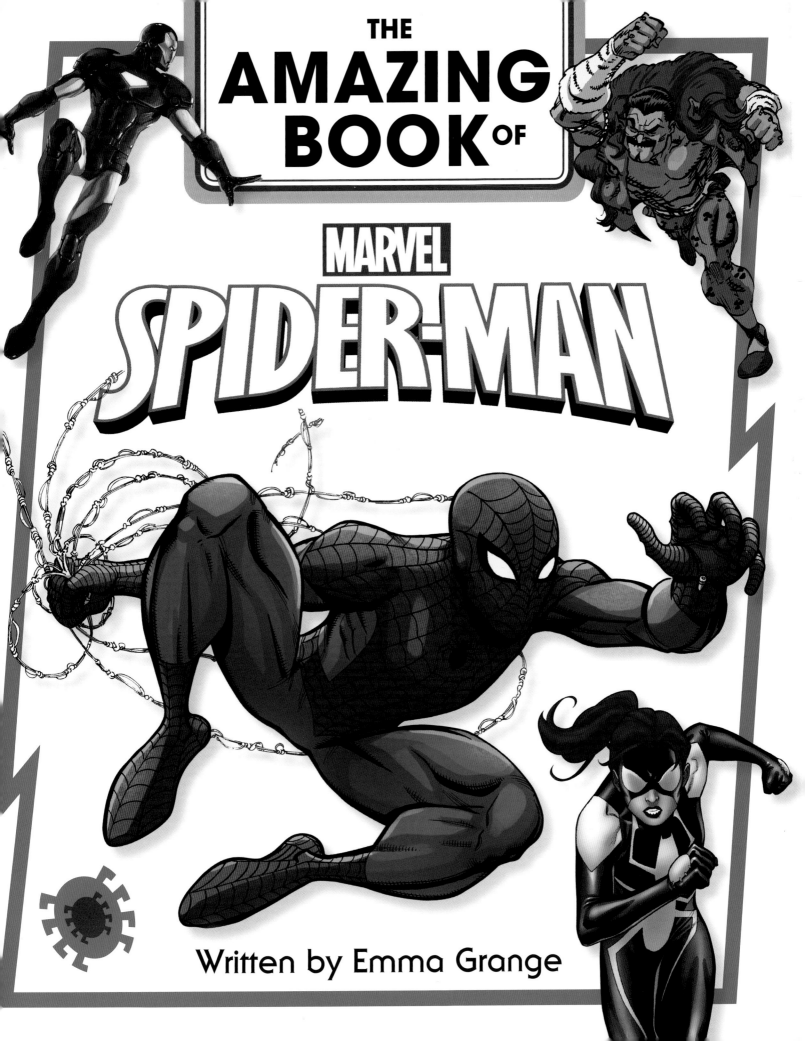

THE AMAZING BOOK OF

MARVEL
SPIDER-MAN

Written by Emma Grange

Introduction

Swing into the neighbourhood of friendly Super Hero Spider-Man. Spidey goes on many adventures. He must often battle fierce foes and common crooks to keep his city safe. Learn all about the amazing web-slinger and his action-packed life!

Look out for **fun questions** throughout the book.

CONTENTS

Glasses worn for studying

Peter Parker

Peter Parker was just an ordinary schoolboy. He had no special powers, although he was very good at science.

What is your favourite subject at school?

Spider's bite

Everything changed for Peter when he was bitten by a radioactive spider. The spider was transformed during a scientific experiment. It gave Peter amazing new powers!

Incredible powers

Peter soon discovered he could jump higher, run faster and hear better than ever before. He decided to become a Super Hero called Spider-Man!

Peter can now jump higher than buildings

Masked identity

To keep his role as Spider-Man secret, Peter made a mask to hide his face. The mask is bright red and webbed like a spider's web.

Eye holes allow Spidey to see

Lift the flap to find out!

What does the rest of my costume look like?

Original design

Spidey's first costume was just a mask worn over his ordinary clothes! To look more like a Super Hero, Peter realised he needed a full-body costume.

Quick change

A Super Hero might be needed at any time. Peter often wears his Spider-Man suit under his clothes so that he is ready to race into action.

T-shirt and jeans worn over Spider-suit

Spider design sits at
centre of costume

Glowing eyes

Boots can withstand lots of running and climbing

Suited up

Peter Parker made his Spider-Man suit himself. The costume is made from stretchy materials. This allows him to swing, climb and jump easily.

If you were a Super Hero, what would your suit look like?

PETER'S FAMILY

Happy home

Peter's parents died when he was young. However, he had a happy childhood, growing up under the care of his Aunt May and Uncle Ben, who loved him very much.

Family times were always full of laughter

Aunt May

Peter knows that Aunt May will always be there for him. She believes that Peter will achieve great things.

Daily Bugle newspaper

Uncle Ben

Peter's Uncle Ben supported Peter at school and at home. He could always give good advice if Peter needed it.

Strong arms for big hugs

Even strong boxers are no match for Spider-Man

Lift the flap to find out!

Which power did I invent in a lab?

Powerful arm muscles

Super strength

Thanks to his spider-like super-powers, Spidey is very strong. He also has good balance and lots of energy.

Wall-crawling

Spider-Man can crawl up walls and across ceilings, just like a real spider! It is a handy way to sneak up on enemies.

Sticky fingers cling to walls

Spidey can even sense a speeding bullet

Spidey sense

Spider-Man's head tingles when danger is near. This is his spider-sense. It gives him time to prepare for action.

Web-slinging

Spider-Man invented a liquid for
making spider webs. He swings
on these webs. He hangs
from them. He even ties his
enemies up in them!

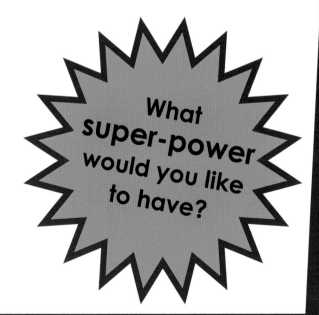

What
super-power
would you like
to have?

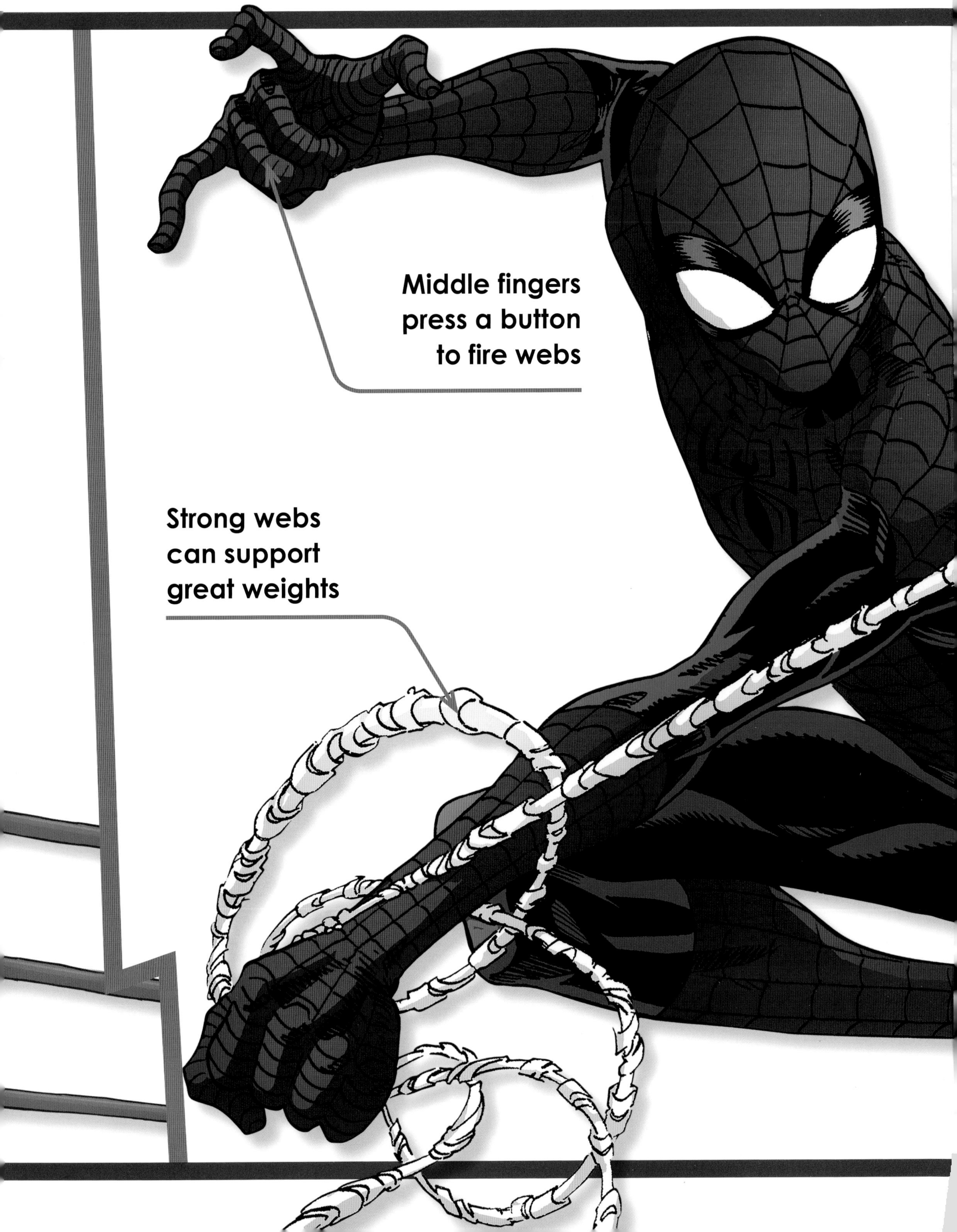
Middle fingers press a button to fire webs
Strong webs can support great weights

Expensive phone paid for by rich father

Harry Osborn

Peter Parker and Harry Osborn became friends at school. Harry's father is the rich and successful, but mean, businessman, Norman Osborn.

Gwen Stacy

Peter Parker met Gwen Stacy when they were both students at Midtown High School. Gwen has no idea that her friend is the Super Hero Spider-Man!

Gwen drags Peter to the library

Mary Jane

Mary Jane Watson is one of the few people that Peter trusts with his Super Hero secret. She sometimes joins Spider-Man on his adventures.

Mary Jane has to hold on tight!

What are your best friends like?

13

THE AVENGERS

The Hulk
Scientist Bruce Banner turns big, green and mean when he is angry. As the Hulk he is incredibly powerful.

Strong legs for leaping

Captain America
Super-strong Captain America leads a Super Hero team called the Avengers. They fight to protect Earth. Sometimes Spider-Man helps them.

Green skin

What would your Super Hero name be?

Armour built by Iron Man

Thor

Fearless warrior Thor is from the planet Asgard. He fights with his indestructible hammer and is almost indestructible himself.

Iron Man

Iron Man can fly or blast his way out of any situation. He wears a high-tech suit of armour. It has many built-in weapons.

Hammer

15

THE DAILY BUGLE

Rolled-up newspaper

Daily news

The *Daily Bugle* reports all of the local news, including who is fighting who. Even Spidey can be spotted reading it!

DAILY BUGLE

NYC'S MOST POWERFUL PEOPLE

Top photographer

Peter Parker has a part-time job working for the *Daily Bugle*. He sells photos of Spider-Man that nobody else can get.

Camera

Mask

Keeping secrets

To keep his family safe, Spider-Man's real identity as Peter Parker remains a secret. Only a few people know the truth.

If you were a **Super Hero**, would you keep it a secret?

How is Peter Parker getting these photos of Spider-Man?

Lift the flap to find out!

J. Jonah Jameson

Grumpy J. Jonah Jameson runs the *Daily Bugle* newspaper. He hates Spider-Man and writes stories that show Spidey as a villain, not a hero.

Spidey's snaps

Peter is able to get such good photos of Spider-Man because he is Spider-Man! He sets up cameras and whizzes past.

Do you like taking photos or writing stories?

Camera worn over shoulder

Smart shirt

Tony Stark
Billionaire Tony Stark is Iron Man! He often gives Spider-Man advice on being a Super Hero and how to keep his secret safe.

American stars and stripes symbols

Steve Rogers
Captain America is really Steve Rogers. His identity is not a secret! He has fought alongside Spider-Man several times and believes that Spidey will make a great hero.

19

Madame Web

Super-powered Madame Web has been a friend of Spidey's for a long time. She uses her ability to see the future to warn him of danger.

Hands can shoot spider webs

Mystical energy blasted from hands

Doctor Strange

Spidey's friend Doctor Strange has magical powers. He often uses these powers, and his ability to fly, to help Spider-Man win fights against his foes.

Black Widow

Black Widow is a trained secret agent and martial artist. She is also a member of the Avengers and often fights alongside Spider-Man.

Bracelets can fire electrical energy bolts

Arrow fired with great accuracy

Hawkeye

He might not have super-powers, but Avengers teammate Hawkeye is a great shot with his bow and arrow. Both he and Spider-Man enjoy making jokes.

Super Villain

This vile, green villain is the Green Goblin. He became extra strong and extra evil after a chemical accident.

Goblin mask worn with green-and-purple costume

Norman Osborn

Surprise! Nasty businessman Norman Osborn is the Green Goblin. By wearing a disguise he can commit crimes without being recognised.

Fierce expression

Business suit

Lift the flap to find out!

What does the Green Goblin look like beneath his mask?

Spidey vs Green Goblin

The Green Goblin is Spidey's greatest enemy. From his Glider, the Goblin is even able to fight Spidey in the air.

Who do you think will win the fight between Spidey and Green Goblin?

Pumpkins

The Green Goblin uses fiery pumpkins for weapons. He hurls them through the air. Watch out, Spidey!

GREEN GOBLIN

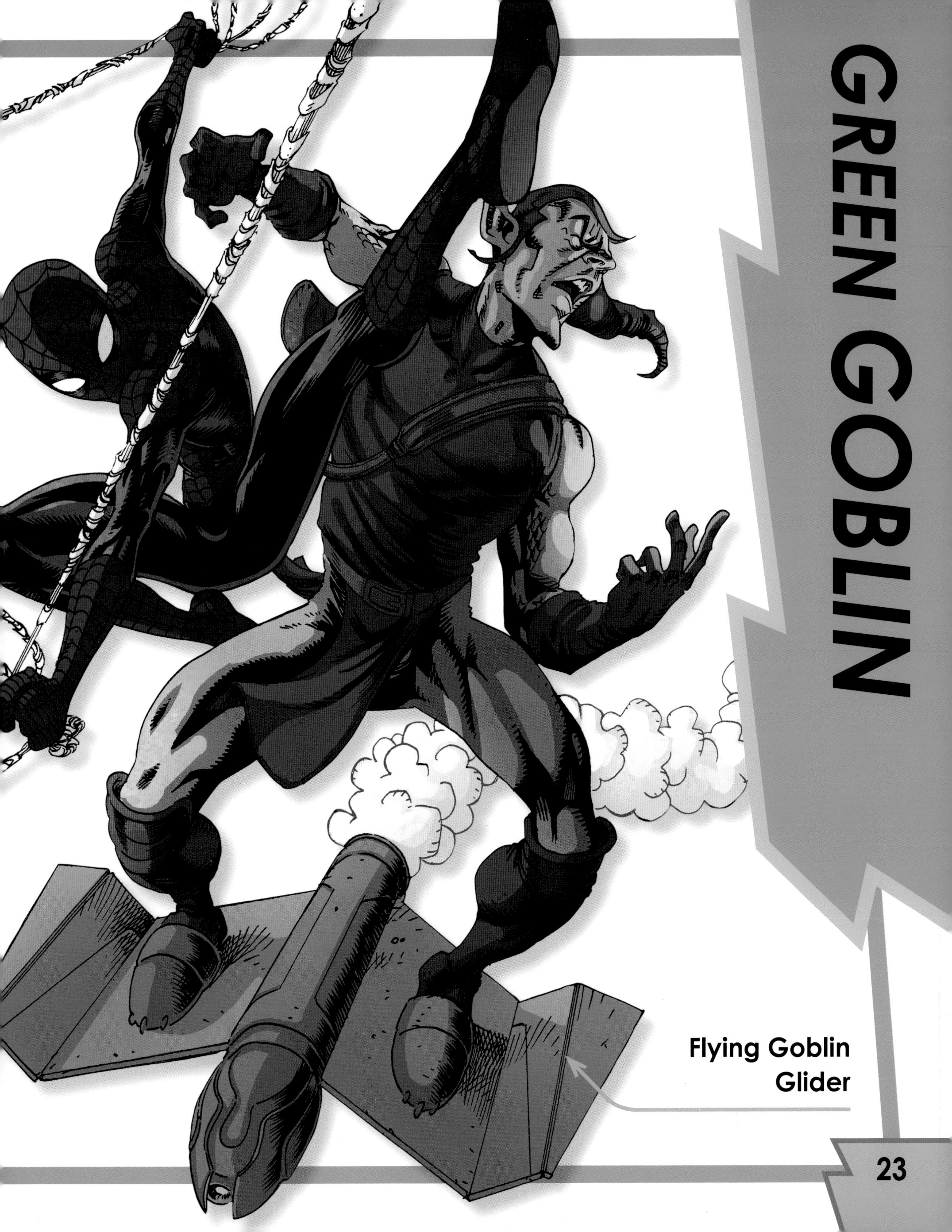
Flying Goblin
Glider

DOCTOR OCTOPUS

Long metal arms can reach objects far away

Super-strong, lightweight metal twists and bends

Doc Ock

Genius scientist Otto Octavius invented robot arms. One day an explosion in his lab resulted in these arms becoming attached to him. Now he is an evil crime lord.

Spidey vs Doc Ock

When Spider-Man fights Doc Ock he must keep out of the way of Ock's long arms! The foe uses them for fighting as well as stealing.

Metal limbs

Doctor Octopus's robotic arms answer only to him. The terrifying tentacles still work even when not attached to their creator.

Pincers for grabbing objects

Lizard limbs can regrow

Lizard

Before he went bad, the Lizard was Spidey's friend. But now he seeks power and wants to make others green and scaly like him.

Scorpion

Powerful blast from tail

The Scorpion was turned into a scary Super Villain so that he could fight Spider-Man. He uses his tail as a weapon.

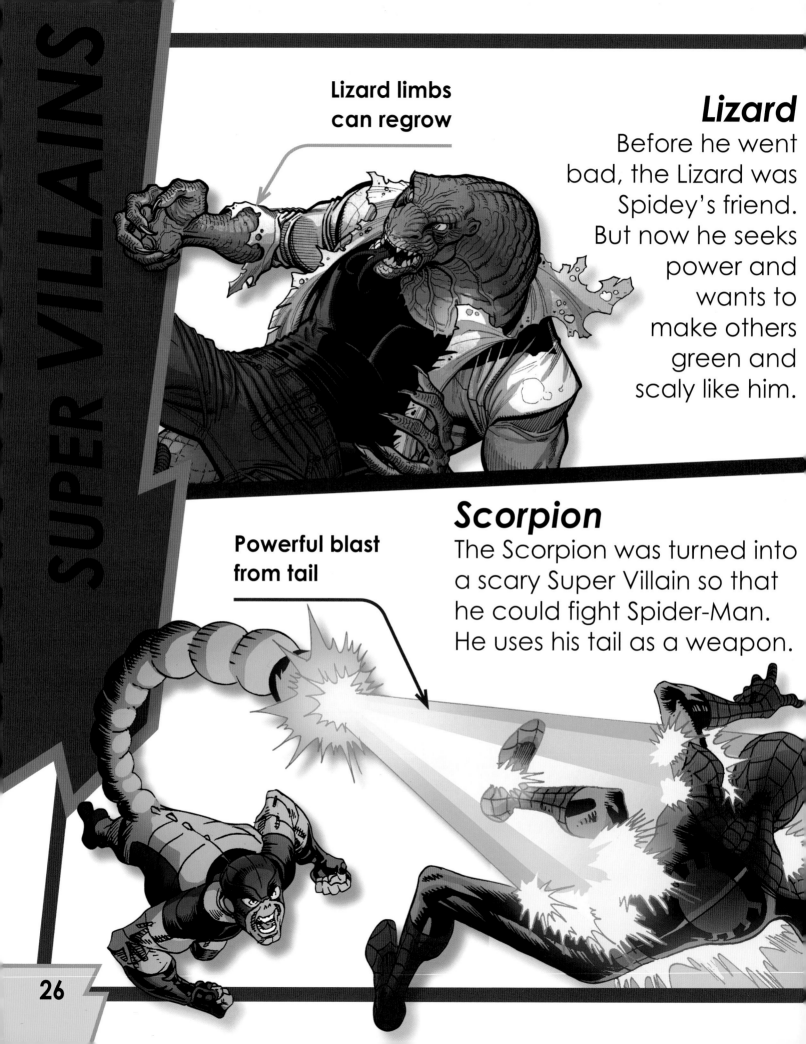

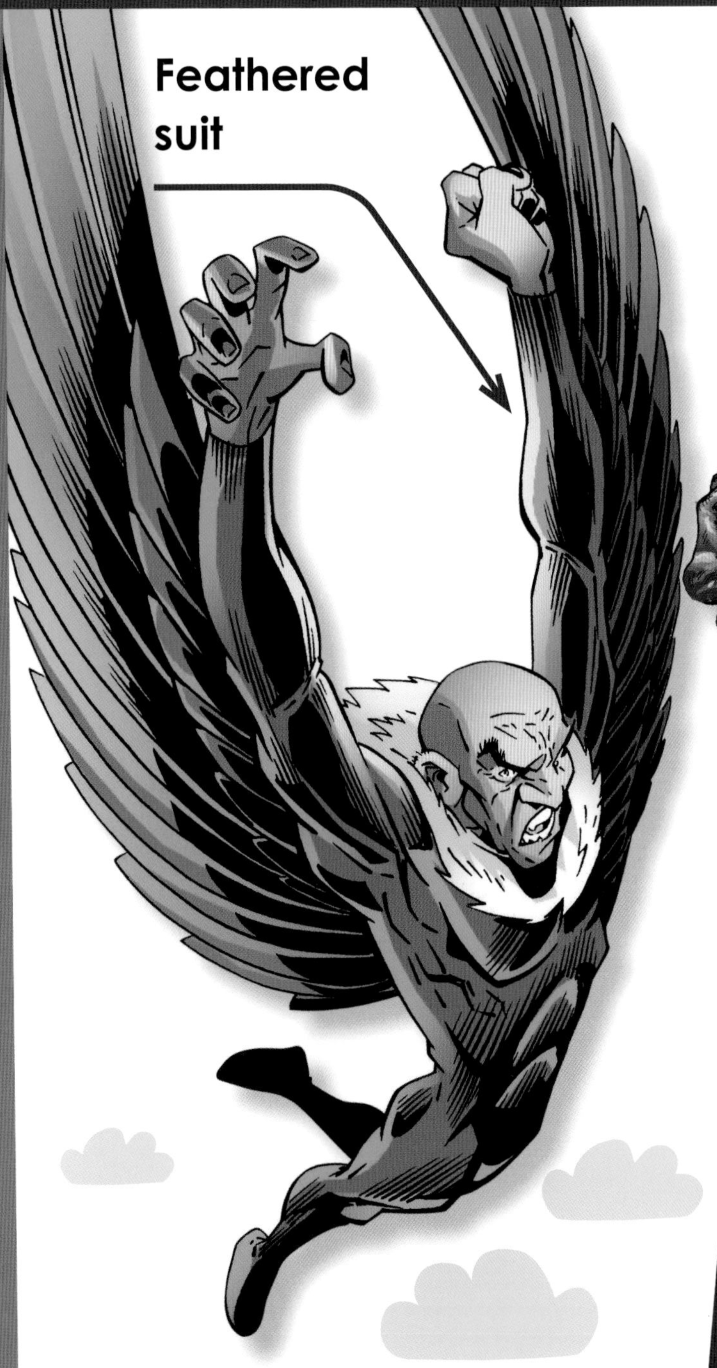
Feathered suit

Vulture

The winged Vulture can attack Spidey from above when wearing his flying suit. Luckily Spidey can take to the skies, too!

Rhino

Rough, tough rogue Rhino is not easy to stop. His super-strong suit allows him to charge through walls and crush cars.

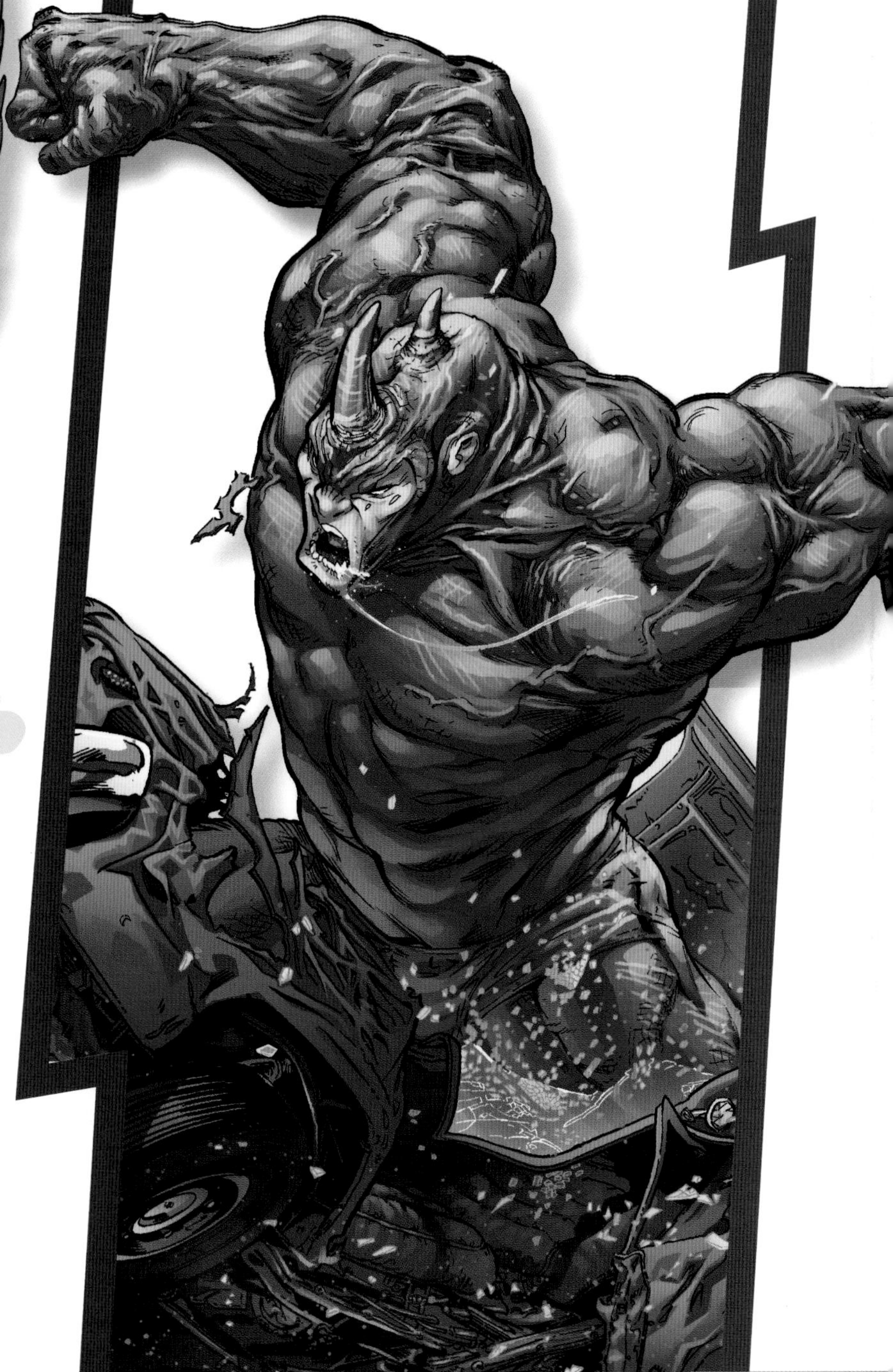

FIENDISH FOES

Kraven the Hunter

Animal-like villain Kraven is obsessed with hunting down Spider-Man. He is as strong and as fierce as a wild beast.

Fur collar

Which shape-shifting villain can turn into sand?

Lift the flap to find out!

Animal-print costume

Chameleon

Guess who? With the Chameleon it's hard to tell, as this foe can pretend to be anyone he chooses.

Mask reveals new disguise

Sandman

The criminal Sandman can grow as big as a house or shrink as small as an ant. He can even turn himself into a sandstorm!

Spider-Man seems tiny next to giant Sandman

How would you **defeat** foes like these?

TOP TEAM UPS

Gauntlets give electric shocks

Shockproof rubber boots

Shocker
This foe broke out of jail after inventing a sonic shock suit. Now he fights Spider-Man as Shocker!

Which Super Hero would you like to work with?

Black cloak for hiding in shadows

Handshake symbolises friendship

Black Panther
The mysterious Black Panther recently asked Spidey for his help. Both are skilled at surprise attacks, so together they make a top pair.

Stretched, extra-large hand

Ms Marvel

As Ms Marvel, Kamala Khan can stretch her body into any shape she likes. She is also quick, so can keep up with speedy Spider-Man.

Lightning-bolt symbol

Black Cat

Spider-Man sometimes works with stealthy burglar Black Cat, but sometimes has to work against her. She can be good or bad, depending on her mood.

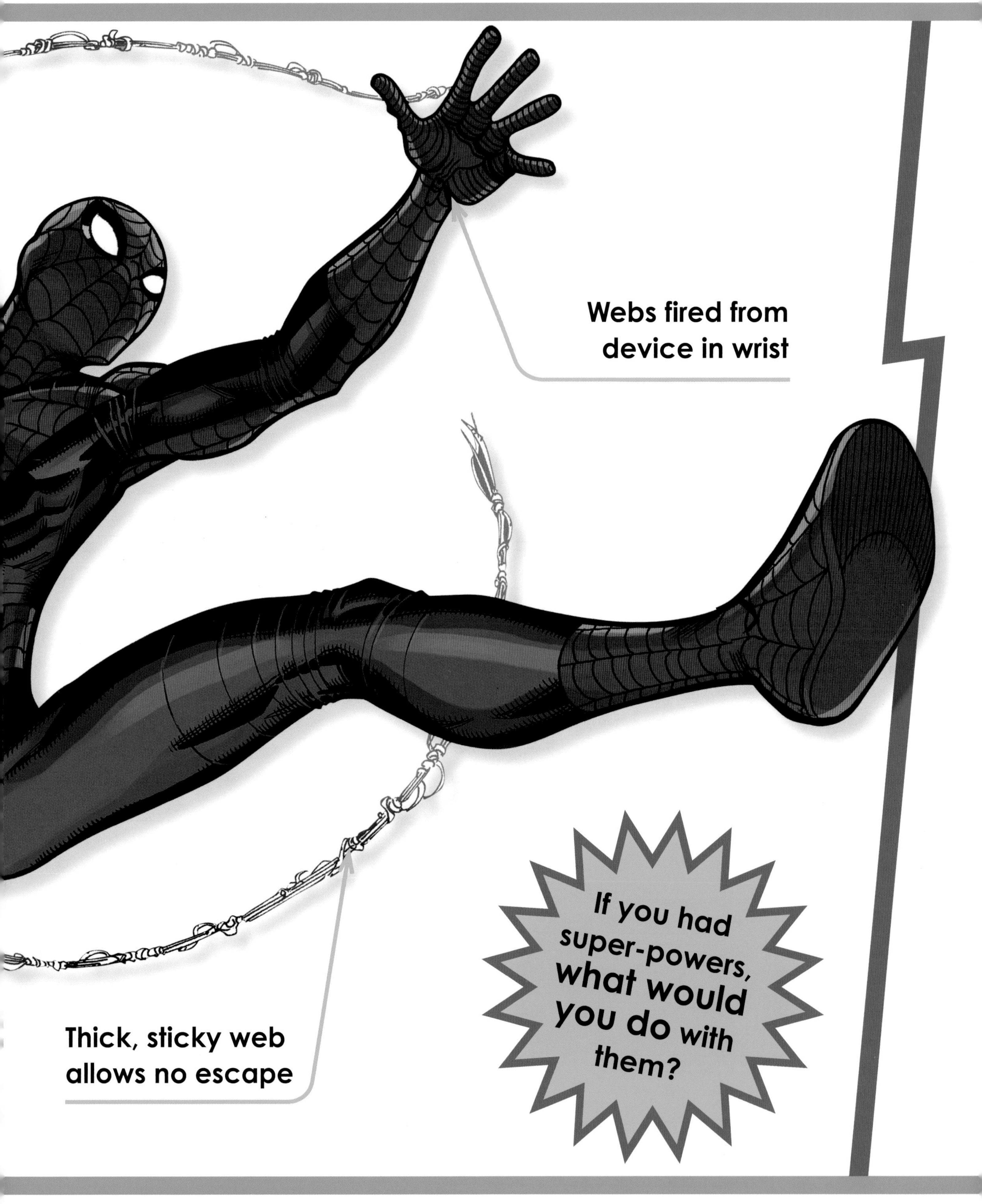
Webs fired from device in wrist
Thick, sticky web allows no escape
If you had super-powers, what would you do with them?

TO THE RESCUE

Fighting foes

Spidey must use all of his super-powers to keep his city safe from danger. Battling villains such as Electro requires speed, strength and agility.

Web can support both Spidey and Gwen

Rescuing friends

Sometimes being a Super Hero puts the people Spidey cares about in danger. He always tries to put his friends, such as Gwen Stacy, first.

OTHER SPIDER-MEN

Unique black-and-red costume design

Webbed cape

Miguel O'Hara
Far into the future, in the year 2099, the mask of Spider-Man is worn by Miguel O'Hara. He fights to continue Peter Parker's good work.

Miles Morales
Peter Parker is not the only Spider-Man! On another version of Earth, 13-year-old Miles Morales is Spider-Man. He has identical super-powers to Peter Parker.

Scarlet Spider

Somebody once created a clone of Peter Parker, making an identical version of Spider-Man. This clone took the Super Hero name Scarlet Spider.

Handy belt for gadgets and weapons

Pockets buckled to ankles

35

Spider-Girl

Anya Corazon is Spider-Girl. She is a hero with spider-like super-powers. She is fast and strong, and as flexible as a gymnast.

Stretchy, elastic-like arms

Would you like to have spider-like powers?

Silk

Cindy Moon was stung by the same spider that bit Peter Parker. As a result, she has the same spidery powers, and uses the Super Hero name Silk.

All tied up

These crooks were robbing a bank when Spider-Man caught up with them. He made quick work of tying them up in spider webs!

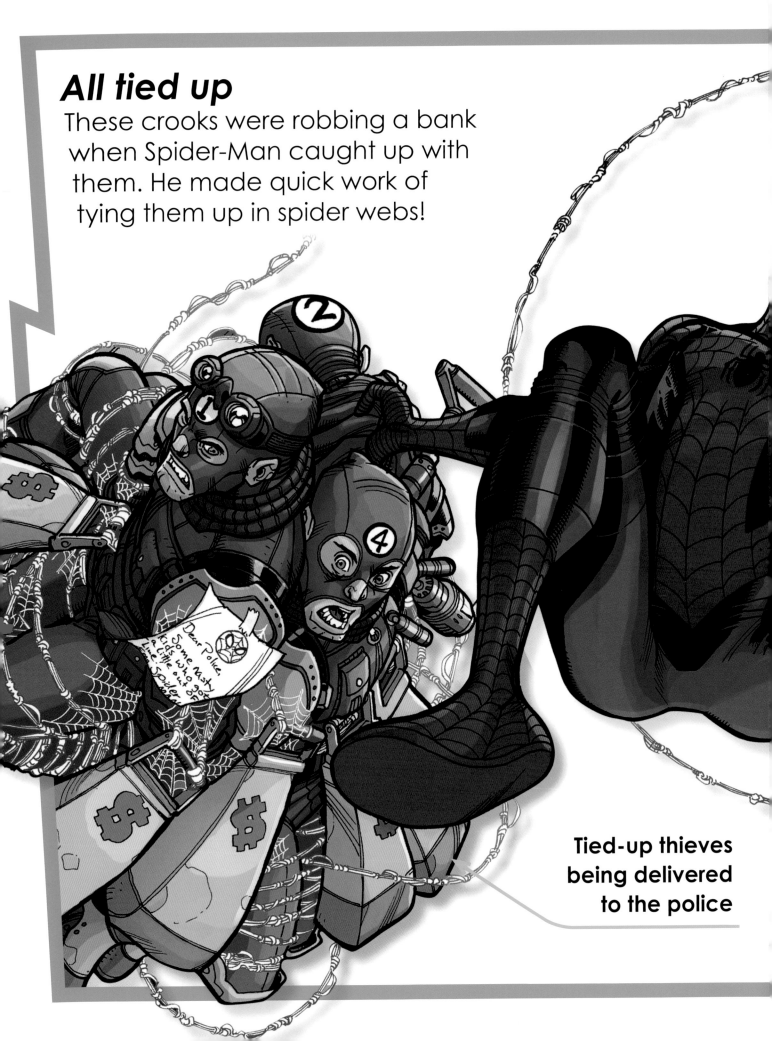

Tied-up thieves being delivered to the police

Chasing robbers

Spider-Man wants to use his powers to do good. As well as battling Super Villains, he is pleased when he can help neighbours and restore justice. This lady was glad when Spidey returned her stolen bag to her.

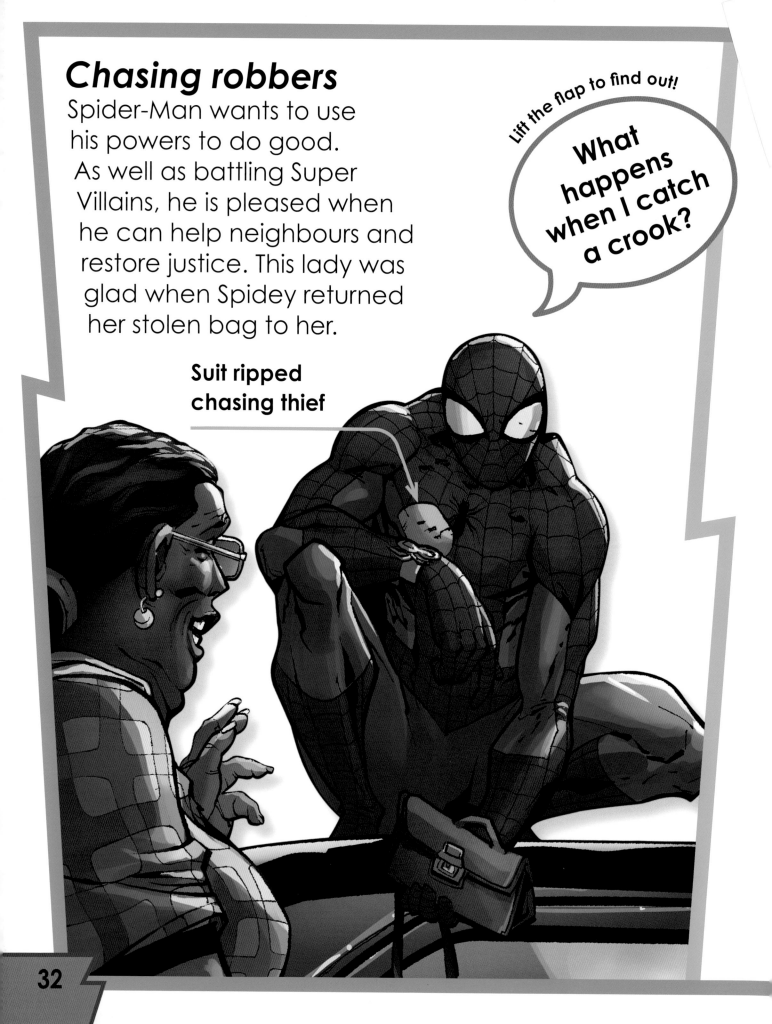

Suit ripped chasing thief

Lift the flap to find out!

What happens when I catch a crook?

Spider Gwen

On another world, it is Gwen Stacy who has super-powers, while Peter Parker is just an ordinary schoolboy!

Webbed hood

Goggles mask face

Spider-Woman

When she was just a baby, an experiment gave Jessica Drew her super-powers. She became Spider-Woman and often partners with Spider-Man to fight crime.

VENOM

Eddie Brock

Eddie Brock hates Spider-Man. When he finds a mysterious alien suit known as Venom, he decides to try it on...

Would you like to wear the Venom suit?

Spidey wearing black Venom suit

Spider Venom

The Venom suit is very strong and has the power to transform people when they wear it. Spider-Man is also strong, but even he struggles to control Venom. When he wears the suit, it nearly turns him bad!

Flash Thompson

Super Hero Flash learned how to use the Venom suit for good. Now when he wears it he fights for justice with the team called the Guardians of the Galaxy.

Venom suit stretches and changes shape

Lift the flap to find out!

What happens when Eddie Brock wears the Venom suit?

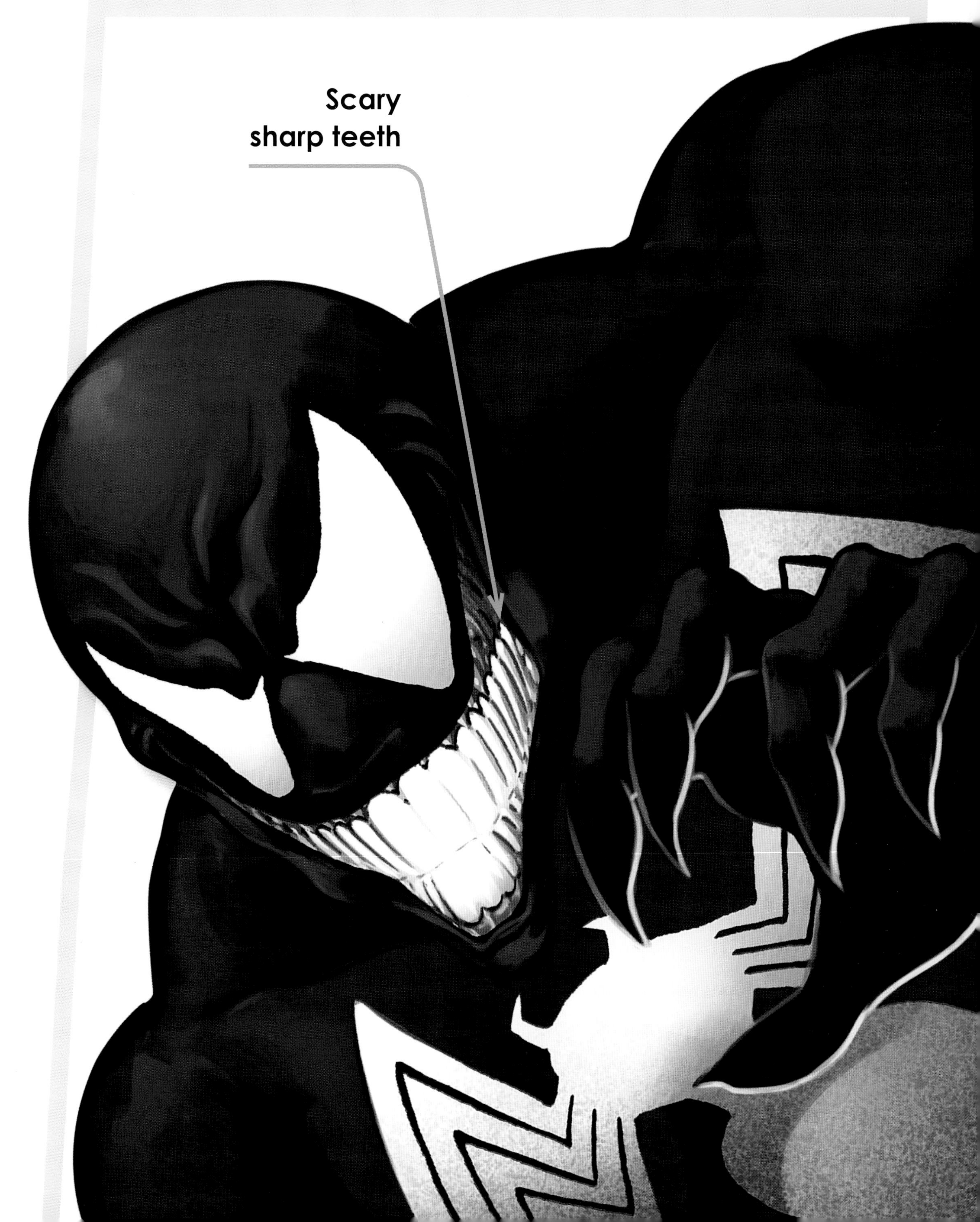
Scary
sharp teeth

Dark suit is good for camouflage

Eddie as Venom

Venom is alive! When Eddie Brock tries on the suit, he turns big and bad and very angry. Now he wants to fight Spidey.

SAVING THE WORLD

Maria Hill

Secret agent Maria works for organisation S.H.I.E.L.D., which protects Earth from danger. Maria and the team think Spidey's skills could be useful to them.

Helicopter can land on top of the Helicarrier

Helicarrier

To save the world from Super Villains, S.H.I.E.L.D. is equipped with many unique vehicles. Its base is a huge armoured aircraft named the Helicarrier.

Nick Fury

Nick Fury is in charge of S.H.I.E.L.D. It is his job to find new Super Heroes, such as Spider-Man, to work with.

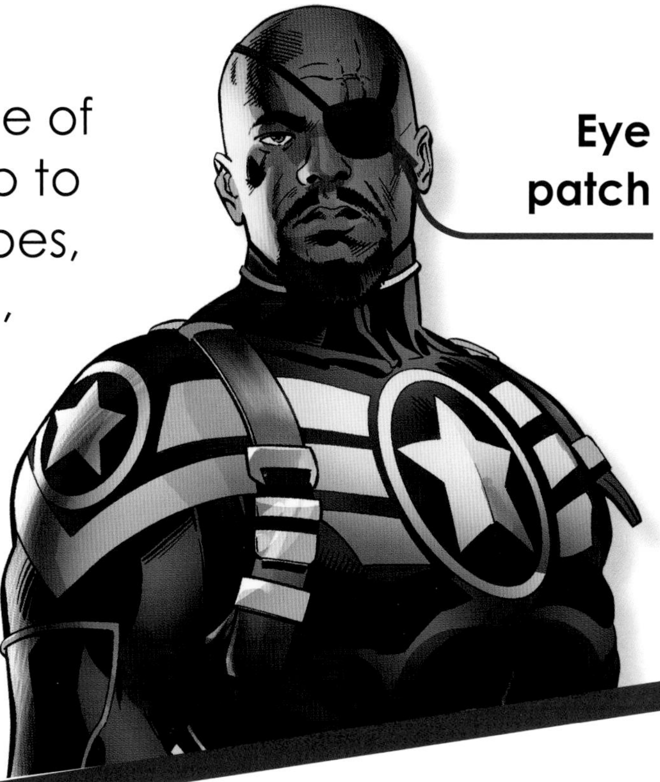
Eye patch

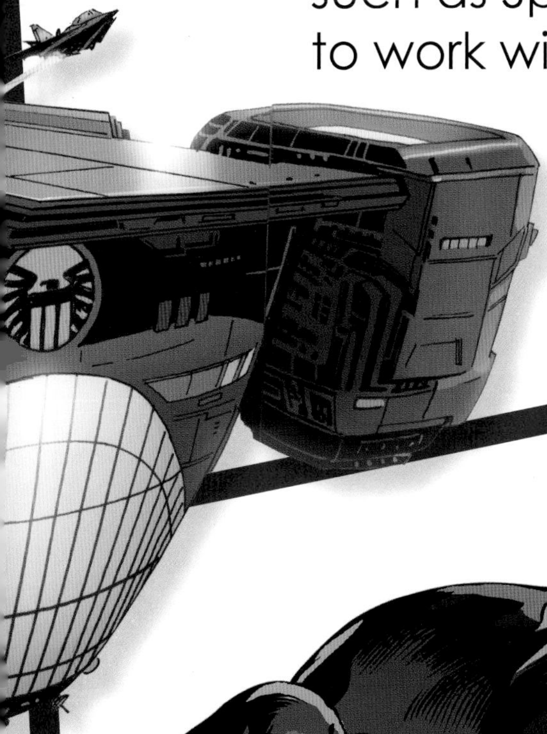

Phil Coulson

Agent Coulson has worked with Spidey on some top-secret missions. He drives a flying red car named Lola.

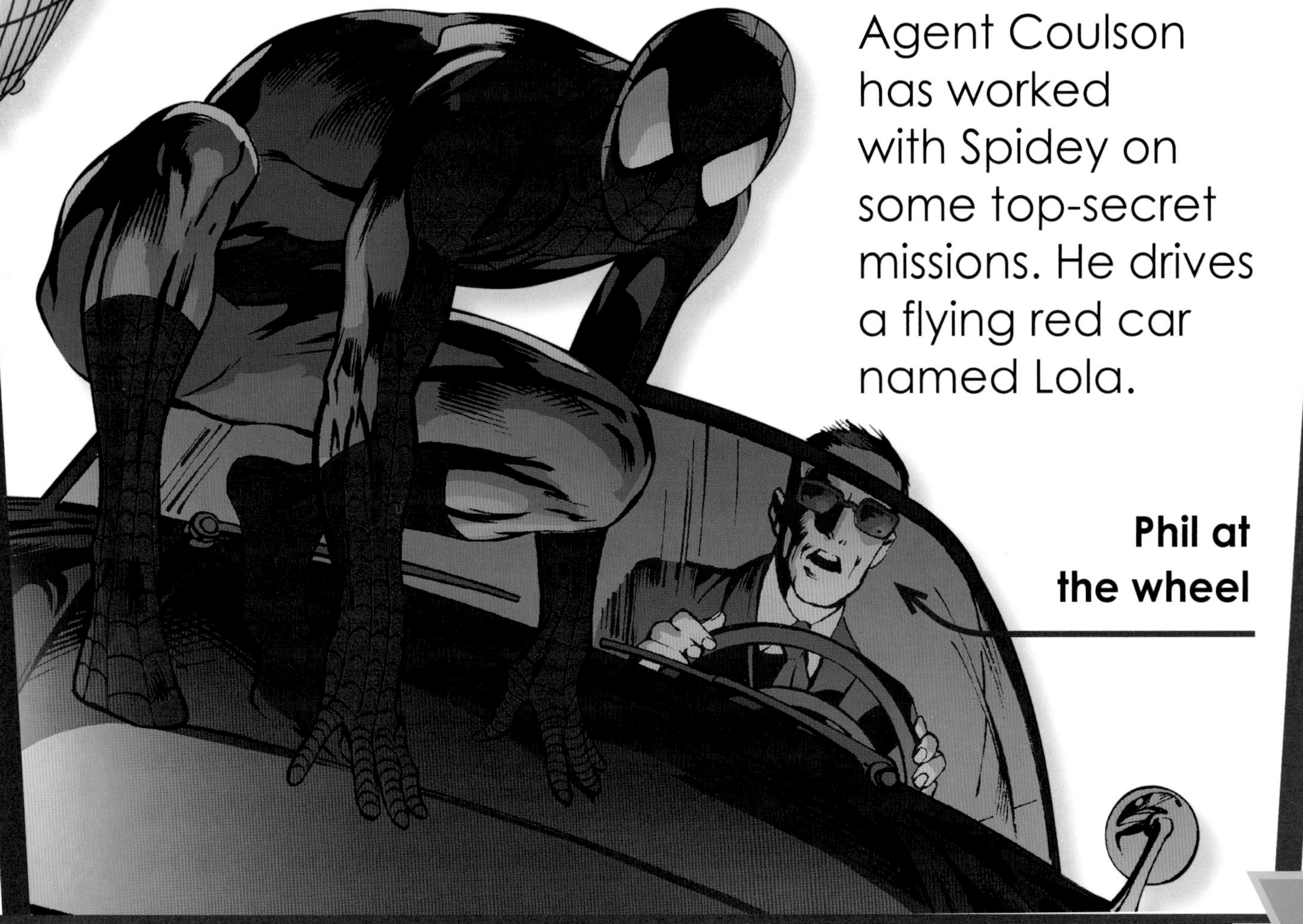
Phil at the wheel

Armoured suit

This silver armoured suit provides Spider-Man with extra protection. However, it also makes him heavier and slower.

Lift the flap to find out!

What suit did Iron Man help me to build?

Metal armour invented by Spidey

Super scientist

Peter Parker is as happy in a lab inventing new gadgets as he is swooping across the city as Spider-Man. He is a talented, experimental scientist.

White lab coat

Spider Mobile

One of Spider-Man's latest inventions is a bright red car full of tricks and extra gadgets. It has web shooters just like he does!

What cool **gadgets** would you like to invent?

Eyepiece cleans itself so never gets dirty

Iron Spider

Iron Man used his own special technology to make this suit with Spider-Man. With built-in gadgets, weapons, communications and a glider, it is Spidey's most multi-functional costume yet.

Red and gold are typically Iron Man colours

Bendy, expandable
arms have sensors

Stealth suit

Can you spot Spidey in his stealth suit? Special material means this costume makes Spidey invisible.

Self-mending material

Large shoulder plate

Battle suit

This extra-chunky suit was built so Spidey could fight extra-large foes such as Rhino. It gives the Super Hero added bulk and protection.

Spider design to scare off foes

Spider-signal

By pressing a button on his utility belt, Spidey can shine a red, spider-shaped light to announce his arrival.

Spider watch

Peter has even used his skills to invent a high-tech watch. With this device he can communicate with others and make telephone calls.

Touch-screen watch face

Wheels can grip to walls and ceilings

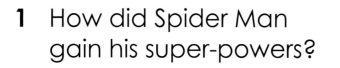

1 How did Spider Man gain his super-powers?

2 What is Spidey's real name?

3 Which version of Spider-Man is this?

4 Which school did Peter Parker go to?

5 What newspaper does Peter Parker work for?

6 What did Otto Octavius invent?

7 Which foe flies on a Goblin Glider?

8 What team, featuring Iron Man and Captain America, does Spidey sometimes help with?

9 What is the name of Peter's aunt?

10 Who is this?

11 Which friend of Spider-Man uses a bow and arrow?

12 Where does Spider-Man keep his web shooters?

13 What is S.H.I.E.L.D.'s flying base known as?

14 What is the name of Phil Coulson's car?

15 Who wears an eye patch?

16 Who can see into the future?

17 Who is this?

18 Which Super Hero name does Jessica Drew use?

19 Which Guardian of the Galaxy wears the Venom suit?

20 Which vehicle has Spidey invented?

You can find the answers on page 48.

Senior Editor Emma Grange
Designers Thelma-Jane Robb, Chris Gould
Design Assistant Abi Wright
Senior Pre-production Producer Rebecca Fallowfield
Senior Producer Zara Markland
Managing Editor Sadie Smith
Managing Art Editor Ron Stobbart
Publisher Julie Ferris
Art Director Lisa Lanzarini
Publishing Director Simon Beecroft

Written by Emma Grange

First published in Great Britain in 2017
by Dorling Kindersley Limited
80 Strand, London, WC2R 0RL
A Penguin Random House Company

10 9 8 7 6 5 4 3 2 1
001–299073–Jun/17

Page design copyright © 2017 Dorling Kindersley Limited

A CIP catalogue record for this book
is available from the British Library

ISBN: 978-0-24128-537-4

DK would like to thank Elizabeth Dowsett for
Anglicisation and editorial assistance.

Printed and bound in China

© 2017 MARVEL

A WORLD OF IDEAS:
SEE ALL THERE IS TO KNOW

www.dk.com

Answers to the quiz
on pages 46 and 47

1 He was bitten by a spider
2 Peter Parker
3 Miles Morales
4 Midtown High School
5 The *Daily Bugle*
6 Robot arms
7 The Green Goblin
8 The Avengers
9 May
10 Black Panther
11 Hawkeye
12 On his wrists
13 Helicarrier
14 Lola
15 Nick Fury
16 Madame Web
17 Sandman
18 Spider-Woman
19 Flash
20 Spider Mobile

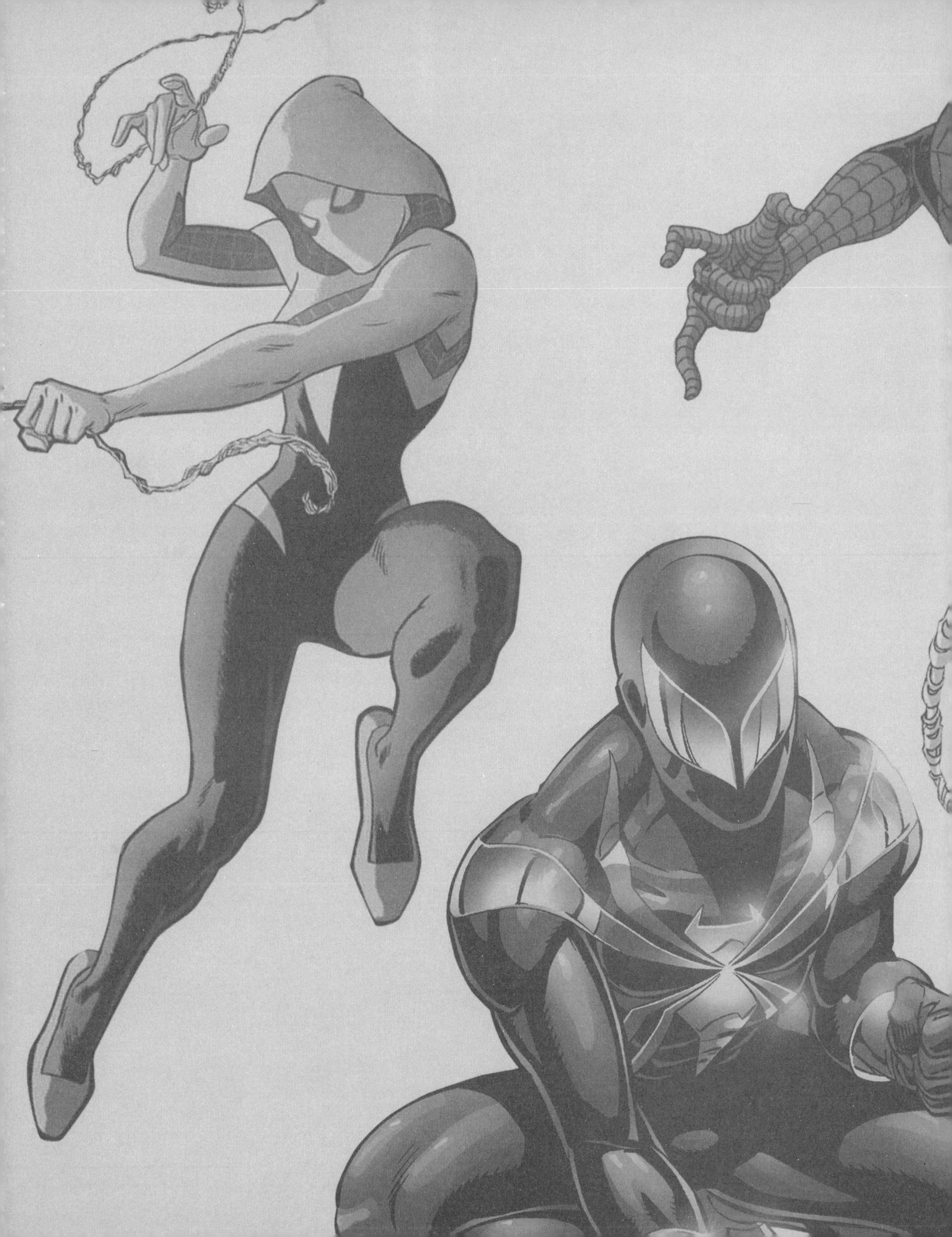